A B  C D 

E  F G  H

I J K  L M

N  O P Q 

 R S  T U

V W X Y Z 

A B  C D 

E  F G  H

I J K  L M

N  O P Q 

 R S  T U

V W X Y Z 

Addicted Animals A to Z

Again for Ariel & Sam

-S.M.

For Aurora & Celeste

-M.O.

Special Thanks To:
Tosca Miserendino
Stacie Odum
Jack W. Perry
Don Loudon
Ron Riffle
Travis Bundy
Shawn Gates
Beverly Miserendino

A PERMUTED PRESS BOOK
ISBN: 979-8-89565-250-3

Addicted Animals A to Z

Illustrated by Mike Odum

Cover art by Mike Odum

This book, as well as any other Permuted Press publications, may be purchased in bulk quantities at a special discounted rate. Contact orders@permutedpress.com for more information.

PERMUTED PRESS

Permuted Press
New York • Nashville
permutedpress.com

Published in the United States of America
1 2 3 4 5 6 7 8 9 10
Printed in Canada

A

If You Give An Alpaca Acid...

B

If You Give A Beaver A Brew...

If You Give A Cow Cocaine...

D

If You Give A Dolphin A Downer...

If You Give An Emu Ecstasy...

If You Give A Fox Fast Food...

CLOWN KING
BABY

If You Give A Gerbil Gin...

H

If You Give A Hedgehog A Highball...

Beer

If You Give An Impala The Internet...

J

If You Give A Jackalope
A Joint...

K

If You Give A Kitten
A Keg...

If You Give A Lemming Librium...

M

If You Give A Monkey A Martini...

N

If You Give A Nightingale Nicotine...

HACK!
HACK!

O

If You Give An Otter Opium ...

P

If A Puppy Plays The Ponies...

FORECLOSURE
FOR SALE

Q

If You Give A Quail A Quaalude...

If You Give A
Raccoon 'Roids...

S

If You Give A Sloth Speed...

If You Give A Tortoise Tobacco...

BEACHRU

U

If You Give A Unicorn Uppers...

If You Give A Vole A Video Game...

Talbott's Tacos
Double Dew
Prince of Pieces

W

If You Give A Whippet
A Whippet...

X

If A Writer And An Artist Try To Come Up With
An Addicted Animal For The Letter X...

Z Z Z
Z Z Z

Y

If You Give A Yeti Your Phone...

INSTACRAM | @RealYeti
ood after a shower
ng #hot #Yetilife
,159
INSTACRAM | @RealYeti
Back to nature. You Only Yeti
Once #YOYO #YetiLife
22,153,159
INSTACRAM | @RealYeti
Kicking it in #LA with fans
#YetiLife
20,028,364
LIVE LIFE LIKE A YETI
#YETILIFE
GOOD TIM
BREAKING
SASQUATCH IS
REAL AND HE'S
GORGEOUS!
Over 300,000,000 FOLLOWERS!
Selfie Star of the Year!

Z

If You Give A Zebra Zinfandel...

ZOO
HOUSE

E N D

And now a word from our sponsors...

D

The letter "D" was brought to you by **Chris Byrne**

S

The letter "S" was brought to you by **Tosca Miserendino**

V

The letter "V" was brought to you by **Matthew Mason**

About the Creators

Author

Sam Miserendino is an attorney by day, author by night, and father 24/7. It was in this latter role that Sam was inspired to write about beer-drinking bunnies and bong-smoking bears. After reading books about carb-addicted moose, mice, and pigs to his son and daughter for the millionth time, Sam's thoughts drifted to other animals and other addictions and so it was that the Addicted Animal Series was born. Sam lives in Buffalo, New York, with his wife, two children, two dogs, and two cats, none of whom, he is happy to report, are addicted to anything more serious than chew toys, catnip, and television.

Illustrator

Mike Odum is an illustrator and former bartender. His experience in both areas informs his skillful renderings of Addicted Animals. When not drawing inebriated mammals, Mike works as a UI/UX Designer and manages to scratch out a small amount of time to develop games for ROOT 76—a game company he co-founded. Mike lives in Richmond, Virginia, with his wife and their two daughters, who enjoy sneaking into his studio and adding their own touches to his work.

GIVE A BEAR A BONG
The Addicted Animal Series

A TO Z

A B  C D 

E  F  G H

I J K L  M

N  O P Q 

 R S T  U

V W  X Y Z

A B C D
E F G H
I J K L M
N O P Q
R S T U
V W X Y Z